MY MAGICAL BROWN UNICORN
SUGAR PIE
and the
MAGIC TRAIL OF POSITIVITY

THIS BOOK BELONGS TO

●●

ISBN: 978-1-7359437-6-3

Library of Congress Control Number: 2021905944

Any references to historical events, real people, or real places are used fictitiously. Names, characters, and places are products of the author's imagination.

Published and Printed in the USA

First printing edition 2021.

Publisher: Royaltee Press LLC

www.royalteepress.com

This book is dedicated to YOU.

You are the best kind of magic

-Ren & Kameryn

MY MAGICAL BROWN UNICORN
SUGAR PIE
and the
MAGIC TRAIL OF POSITIVITY

Written by **Ren and Kameryn Lowe**

Illustrated by **Zeynep Zahide Cakmak**

Today is just not my day! Nothing seems to be going my way.
My ponytails are big and fluffy, but I wanted them to be smaller.
My favorite dress is too little, because I grew taller.

I wanted to go outside and play, and feel the warm sun beaming down on my skin. But guess what? It's raining, and I can't find my raincoat! So now I have to stay in!

Good thing I didn't misplace my magical headband. I'd be so disappointed if I couldn't see Sugar Pie, she's my very best friend.

I put on my headband, and wait for her magical entrance.
Her glitter and sparkles I can see from a **distance** .

The moment Sugar Pie looked at my face she knew that I wasn't my normal **sprightly**, **sparkling** self.

"What's wrong?", asked Sugar Pie "How can I help?"

"Well, my hair isn't quite right, I can't go outside to play, and look at my outfit, it just won't do! But, I'd feel much better if I went on a magical adventure with you".

Sugar Pie smiled so **pleasantly**. She had the perfect place just for me. We were headed to The Magic Trail of Positivity.

Read out loud

The magic trail of positivity

There was just one rule. I had to read out loud
every sign that I see.

To show me how it should be done, Sugar Pie said she would read the very first one. I could tell from the way that the trail was glowing, this adventure was going to be fun!

You are unique!

"You are unique, you are one of a kind, and on the cloudiest of days you still shine"

I am talented, I am fashionable, I have my own style, whatever I wear I'm sure to wow.

Intelligent

I am important

I have a beautiful mind, I am brilliant, I am smart, and I complete whatever I start.

I am goodness, I am important, I matter, and I am loved,
my self esteem floats as high as the stars above.

Brilliant

I am intelligent, I am sassy, sweet like sugar, and
bold like spice I am above average,
I am ALL things great, I am the
definition of nice!

As we moved along the trail, I began to see that all of the signs were filled with words of positivity. I began to feel much better about myself and my day, speaking these positive words were wiping my **frustration** away!

"You're a great student, You're a great leader, and a great teacher too, there is so much magic inside of you".

I can do anything I put my mind to! I am brave, and I am courageous, I am fun, and my smile is **contagious!**

You are creative, you try new things, you have a brilliant mind, and you are helpful.

I am confident, I am strong, I am truthful, and I am respectful.

I couldn't wait to reach the next sign, positive thoughts were running through my head. But there was no other sign. There stood a beautiful unicorn instead. It was all Black, and had a shiny Golden **alicorn** with Silver and Gold **dreads** !

It was Sugar Pie's cousin, Lightning! What a wonderful surprise! She had told me stories about him, and now he was standing right before my eyes.

"Hi Kam, it's nice to meet you.
I heard your day started out kind of rough."

"Yes, but then I began to walk the trail and remembered...
I am patient, I can face any challenge, I am resilient,
and I am enough!

I like me just the way I am, I'll never give up, I'll always try.
aannddd... I also know that you are beautiful Lightning...
and different, just like me and Sugar Pie!

Lightning Replied, "Just remember that these are not just words, everyone of them is true! The same way that you believe in me and Sugar Pie. We also believe in you!"

Sugar Pie and Lightning smiled and gave each other a wink. The Magic Trail of Positivity was indeed a success! When you think positive thoughts, there's no room for gloominess.

I was no longer upset, my frustration had gone away.
All it took was some positivity to brighten up my day.

So if YOUR day is not going the way you
planned it, or you're feeling kind of sad.
STOP and READ these words out loud.

I am ABSOLUTELY POSITIVE...
That this is going to be the best day I've ever had!

Whimsical Words

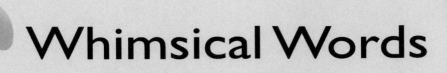

Beaming   : To shine brightly

Distance   : The amount of space between
                   two things or people

Sprightly   : Full of spirit and energy

Pleasantly   : In an enjoyable or friendly way

Positivity   : Thinking good thoughts, and having
                   a good attitude

Frustration   : Being upset or annoyed because
                   you are unable to do something

Contagious   : Able to be passed from one person
                   to another through contact

Alicorn   : A Unicorn's Horn

Dreads   : A narrow ropelike strand of hair

Resilient   : Being able to overcome challenges

A Message From The Authors

My Magical Brown Unicorn is more than just a book series. It is a mindset. One that Authors Ren and Kameryn Lowe desire for all of their readers to have. Which is embracing your uniqueness. You don't see many Magical Brown Unicorns represented in books or cartoon animations, which means that they (we) are very rare. Being a Magical Brown Unicorn means that YOU are unique and truly one of a kind, so beautiful and of course MAGICAL!! This mindset and ideal is one that both authors hope will transcend beyond what we look like on the outside, and also focus on highlighting our magic within.

We hope that you have enjoyed book number 2 in the My Magical Brown Unicorn series. Make sure to follow us on all of our social media platforms to stay updated on all of our new releases!

Connect with the authors by visiting:

www.royalteepress.com
Instagram: @RenLoweAuthor @Kams_Kronicles
@Royalteepress_
Email: Info@royalteepress.com

Made in United States
Orlando, FL
19 February 2022

14972536R00022